PLAGUE HOUSE

"Look at this," Jenna said, and I saw that beside the bedstead, propped up on to a low shelf, was a jagged piece of mirror about a metre long. A lot of its silvering had gone and it was dark and spotted with age.

"It's just a bit of mirror," I said.

"No, I think it's more than that," she said in a strange voice. "Or less. . ."

"What're you talking about? What d'you mean?"

"Look – it doesn't show my reflection."

"*What?*"

"I can't see me in it. Instead I can—" She suddenly gave a piercing scream and jumped backwards.

"What's the matter *now*?" I asked, going up behind her and trying to see what it was that she'd seen in there.

"I saw someone *else's* face staring at me!" she said, sounding terrified. "It was another girl. Not me at all."

Look out for:

Haunted House

PLAGUE HOUSE

MARY HOOPER

■ SCHOLASTIC

For Richard, again

Scholastic Children's Books,
Commonwealth House, 1–19 New Oxford Street,
London, WC1A 1NU, UK
A division of Scholastic Ltd
London ~ New York ~ Toronto ~ Sydney ~ Auckland
Mexico City ~ New Delhi ~ Hong Kong

First published in the UK by Scholastic Ltd, 2004

Copyright © Mary Hooper, 2004

ISBN 0 439 97724 X

Printed and bound by Nørhaven Paperback A/S, Denmark

10 9 8 7 6 5 4 3 2 1

The right of Mary Hooper to be identified
as the author of this work has been asserted by her in
accordance with the Copyright, Designs and Patents Act, 1988.

CHAPTER ONE

"That's disgusting," I said, peering over the fence into the yard of the Murray's farm, the floor of which was completely covered in something thick and brown and smelly. "What is it?"

"Slurry," Jenna said.

"Errrlerrch! It smells revolting and it sounds revolting. What's slurry?"

"Well, basically," said my sister, "it's poo. Cow's poo."

"How d'you know that?"

She shrugged. "It's just one of those things you find out when you're living in a place like this."

"Yeah," I said resignedly, "I s'pose you do."

A place like this was Bensbury, which was a small village miles from anywhere. Miles from shops, swimming pools, buses, friends and football. Miles from life as we knew it. We hadn't wanted to come, but Mum had taken over the running of the local post office and general store, so we'd had to. The three of us were living in rooms right above it so Jenna and I were available – *too* available – to help out in the shop and deliver parcels and stuff to people in the village. That morning we'd had to lug a boxed-up bit of machinery to Murray's Farm, just outside the village.

Jenna and I both hated it in Bensbury. That went without saying. I hated it because I'd had to leave all my mates behind, because there was nothing to do, nowhere to go and no one to go with even if there had been. I especially hated it because there were no football pitches; and the village green, the only reasonable grassy space near us, had a sign on it saying *No Ball Games*. I'd knocked down this sign (with a ball, natch) as soon as I could, but it had been put up again almost overnight.

"*Slurry*," I said now, making the word sound as disgusting as possible. "You only get stinking things like *slurry* in the country."

"Exactly." Jenna sniffed the air – a deep sniff –

and then started coughing and choking. "Yuck! It's what Mum would call a fresh farmyard smell."

"Yeah. Right," I said.

After we'd delivered the box we began walking back to the village. When we'd got a fair distance from the farm – and well away from the slurry – I began dribbling my football down the lane, doing a few keepy-ups along the way. "So, what shall we call the Murrays?" I asked, jerking my thumb back to indicate the farm we'd left. We had this game going to help us memorize the locals' names; we gave them nicknames which had a similar sound to their own surnames according to what they looked like or what they did. We already had Ratty Ratcliffe (small woman with rodent's face) Grouchy Green (old chap, always moaning) and Bumface Butley (need I say more?) and a load of others.

Jenna looked thoughtful. "What's Mr Murray's number one characteristic?"

"His bigness and fatness," I said promptly. We'd been amazed and dumbstruck when he'd opened his front door and filled up the doorway like an overweight carthorse.

"But we've already got a load of fat ones,"

Jenna said. "Piggy Pinder, Mrs Huge-o Hugo and Fatty Fraser. . ."

"What else is there about him, then?" I said, frowning. "What about him being as bald as a coot?"

"We've already got Slaphead Slade," Jenna pointed out.

I suddenly grinned. "There's always the slurry. What about Slurry Murray?" ·

"Cool!" Jenna nodded.

We walked further on and I gave my ball a fair whack down the lane. A great kick, it was – forty metres easily. I was about to sprint after it when I realized Jenna had stopped and was just standing in the lane with a funny look on her face, her eyes half-closed.

"Does it seem weird to you round here?" she asked.

"Too right!" I said.

"No, I don't mean Bensbury itself – we already know that's weird. I mean right *here*."

There was something in the way she said it which kept me from going after the ball straight away. Jenna sometimes gets these feelings, you see, these supernatural, psychic sorts of feelings where she senses things. It had been her who'd started us off ghost-hunting in the village – she'd seen a dog that wasn't really there, and then she'd seen the ghost of someone being murdered a hundred years ago. And now – well, it might seem downright odd to take notice of what your younger sister said (I was older by two and a half minutes) but sometimes, just occasionally, I did.

"You mean weird in a spooky way?" I asked.

She nodded. "There's just something. . . I dunno." She stared across the field, squinting her eyes towards a group of dark trees in the distance. "It's strange. . . Look at this field; it looks neglected, somehow, the grass is all stunted and yellowish." She pointed to the trees. "And that little wood there – does it look kind of *brooding* to you?"

"Ummm. . ." I frowned, staring at the wood. The trees didn't look brooding to me, they just looked quite ordinary. Green with branches. Like trees always were. I wasn't going to miss the opportunity for a bit of spookiness, though, considering it was the only fun we had round here. "Yeah. See what you mean," I lied.

I ran ahead to retrieve my ball, then leaned on the five-bar gate which led into the field, waiting for Jenna to catch me up. She appeared at my side and just stood there, staring over the gate. "What's different about this field? What do you see?" she asked.

"Grass," I said. This so obviously wasn't the right answer that I added, "A field that would make a decent-sized football pitch."

She ignored that. "No, there's something more. Apart from the look of it, there are no birds singing, no insects flitting about or bees buzzing, and the whole place seems . . . flat, somehow. Dead."

I lifted the latch and pushed the gate open. "Mum's not expecting us back," I said. "If you think there's something weird about it here, let's go in and have a look round."

I steadied my ball, gave it a mighty thwack through the open gate, then sprinted after it. When I turned, ready to chip it back, Jenna hadn't moved. She was just standing by the boundary hedge with the same dippy look on her face.

I brought the ball back and expertly dribbled it around her.

"Stop doing that a minute," she said suddenly. "I can hear something."

I listened, but couldn't hear anything.

"It's coming from those trees," she said.

"What is?"

"Singing."

I laughed a bit scornfully. "Right! What sort of singing? R&B? Country and Western? Slurry Murray rapping?"

She tilted her head to one side. "Not that sort of singing. It's children's voices and they're singing. . ." She screwed up her face. "You're going to think I'm making this up."

"Try me."

"They're singing, 'Ring a Ring o' Roses'. . ."

I burst out laughing.

"Maybe there's a house somewhere, hidden from view," she said.

We looked all around and tried to peer through the trees, but couldn't see anything.

"We'll ask in the village," I said. With a bit of luck it could be another cracking spook mystery to investigate. . .

"Glad you're home," Mum said when we arrived back at the shop fifteen minutes or so later. "This packet's just arrived for Mr Adams, and I need you to take it round."

I shook my head slightly at Jenna not to say

7

anything about the field and the mysterious singing. Mum has been known to go into one if she thinks we're up to anything we shouldn't be.

"Mr Adams? Never heard of him," I said.

"No, I don't think he's been in the shop yet," Mum said. "So you'll be extra nice when you take his letter round, won't you? We want everyone in the village to become customers of ours."

I gave her a look. "I don't *do* nice," I said witheringly.

Jenna and Mum both burst out laughing. "Oh, you're so cool, bruv," Jenna said. Mum passed me the packet we had to deliver, which had a blue *Registered* sticker on it. The label was addressed to Mr Adam Adams and I pointed this out to Jenna and we decided it was probably the most unimaginative name we'd ever heard.

"Bet he's really boring," I said.

"Where does he live?" Jenna asked.

I looked at the address. "Two Meadow View," I said. "Isn't that next to Stuffer Starr?" Stuffer was one of the most peculiar people we'd come across so far; a taxidermist who made a living from stuffing people's pets when they passed to that great boarding kennel in the sky.

"I think it *is* next to Mr Starr," Mum said. "And both of you, please be careful that no one else in the village hears you using those nicknames you've made up. Some people might not like what you've chosen."

Jenna and I exchanged glances. Obviously no one would like the names we'd chosen; that was the whole point of them.

Outside the post office, Major (Bumface) Butley was just tying up his black Labrador, Mutton. We stopped to pat Mutton and I gave Jenna the nod to ask a couple of questions. She's better with wrinklies than I am.

"Major Butley," she began politely, "Jake and I were wondering about that field near Murray's farm. Does anyone live near there? Anyone with children?"

Bumface looked at us. "*What?*" he barked.

"That field near Murray's farm," Jenna repeated.

"The one with the group of trees in the middle," I added.

Major Butley's fat, red face grew a little redder. "You don't want to go near that place!" he said.

"But we thought we heard children there," Jenna put in. "Children singing nursery rhymes.

We wondered if there was a house nearby that we couldn't see."

"You didn't hear any singing!" Bumface said gruffly. "Wind in the trees, more like. Or your imagination. You stay away from there."

"Why?" I asked.

"Because," was all he said. And there's nothing quite so aggravating as someone saying *that*.

"But why should we stay away?" I persisted.

"Never you mind. You just keep away from Corpses' Copse," he said. "It's no place for you. No place for anyone." And saying that, he shouted "Stay!" to Mutton and went into our post office, crashing the door behind him so hard that the glass shook.

Jenna and I looked at each other. "What d'you think?" she asked.

"Corpses' Copse?" I said. "Sounds like our sort of place. You up for it?"

"You bet."

"Soon as we can. This week for def," I added as we carried on round the green towards Mr Adams's cottage.

"I wonder what we'll call this Mr Adams," Jenna said. "I hope he's got something funny about him."

"Living here?" I said. "Of course he will."

Just as we'd thought, his cottage was next door to Stuffer Starr's and though it was identical in size and shape, it looked tatty. It didn't have any flowers in the front garden, only a straggle of nettles and weeds, and there were old black curtains pulled right across the front windows. The man himself wasn't in, but, having nothing else to do, we banged and banged on the door until a woman came out of the cottage on the other side and stood there shaking her head at us.

"Who's this?" I said in an undertone to Jenna.

"Can't remember," she said, and then the woman spoke and we knew immediately that it was Miss Squires – better known as Squeaker Squires.

"There's no point in you banging the door like that," she said to us in a shrill, high voice. "Mr Adams has been away for three weeks and no one knows where he is. He's disappeared off the face of the earth!"

"We've got this package for him," I said. "It's registered and someone's got to sign for it."

"Would you take it in for him?" Jenna asked.

"Ooh, no," the woman squeaked. "Don't want to get involved, me. You take it back to the post office."

"Perhaps Stuff— Perhaps Mr Starr will take it in," I said to Jenna.

The woman laughed – or squealed, I should say. "No, he won't!" she said. "They're enemies, those two. Can't stand each other."

"OK," I shrugged. "We'll take it back with us."

Squeaker went indoors again, and we left Mr Adams's and walked back past Stuffer's cottage which, unfortunately, had thick net curtains that prevented us from looking in. I was dying to have a nose in there; I was sure it would be full of stuffed bears and wildebeest.

"Wonder what he's stuffing at the moment," Jenna said. "It was squirrels last time."

Something funny occurred to me. "Wonder if he does anything really big?" I said.

"What – like elephants?"

"No," I said. "Like people."

"*What?!*"

"Well," I said, grinning, "Think about it. Mr Adams disappears mysteriously. He and Stuffer hate each other, and Stuffer stuffs things. Living in a place like this, what are we supposed to think?"

"You're crazy!"

"Maybe I am," I said, "and maybe I'm not. . ."

CHAPTER TWO

A couple of days later when I was slumped in the back room of the shop watching a cartoon on TV, Mum called through for me to go and open the shop door for Squeaker Squires.

Lost the use of her hands, has she? I thought to myself, but I came out all the same and opened the door with an exaggerated flourish.

"Good morning, Mrs Squires!" I said. I lifted her shopping trolley over the step and spotted that it was full of cleaning products. "Are you going to make everything *squeaky* clean?" I asked her.

"What's that?" she squealed, and I heard a giggle from Jenna. She got this under control, then said politely, "Has Mr Adams come back yet, Mrs Squires?"

Squeaker shook her head. "He's gone for good, if you ask me," she said in her funny high voice. "No sign of him – he left no note, nothing. I had to stop his milk and newspapers myself."

Jenna and I exchanged raised-eyebrow looks at this, and I pictured the unknown, immobile Mr Adams stuffed to perfection, standing in one of those huge glass cases you sometimes see dead fish in. Wow! What if he was. . .

"But I can't stand here gossiping all day. Thank you and good morning!" she squealed as she trundled off.

"Nice squeaking to you," I called after her politely.

"Jake!" Mum said as I closed the door. "The poor woman can't help how she speaks." Her mouth twitched a bit. "Or should I say, how she *squeaks*."

"See!" I said. "You tell *us* off. . ."

Mum sat down on her stool behind the post office counter. "Now, what are you two doing with yourselves today?" she asked in the bracing sort of voice she'd been using with us since we'd been living in Bensbury.

"Oh, I thought I'd play a game of five-a-side with the boys and then we'd go skateboarding, and after that just hang out in town," I said, describing what used to be my favourite sort of day.

She pretended not to hear. "Why don't you both go for a nice walk?"

"Yeah, brilliant," I said. "We could have a nature ramble."

"Lovely!" Mum said, and then she looked at me and realized I was joking.

Jenna gave me a look. "We *could* go on a bit of a ramble," she said. "We could go to that field – the one near Slurry Murray's farm. *You know.*"

I'd caught on to what she was getting at. "The one with Cor— the group of trees in the middle?" I said. "Yeah, we could do."

Mum nodded, looking at us both with satisfaction. "Well, I'm pleased you're making use of the countryside at last," she said. "If it continues, I could buy you some books on wild birds and flowers for your birthdays. That'd be nice, wouldn't it?"

Jenna and I turned to her in outrage, but saw by the look on her face that it was her idea of a joke...

* * *

"OK," Jenna said when we were walking along the lane towards the field, "I didn't want to talk about this while Mum was around, but while you were vegging out in front of the telly I was looking things up. Reading more about that nursery rhyme."

"What about it?"

"Well, I knew there was something about it . . . Mrs Ditcham did it when we were learning about the great plague at school. Can't you remember?"

I frowned, trying to think. My brain was generally full right up with Premiership players, what positions they played in and what clubs they played for, so there was never much room for anything else.

"OK, I'll tell you," Jenna said. "'Ring a Ring o' Roses' dates from the time of the great plague in the seventeenth century."

"Mmm. . ."

She frowned. "Show a bit of interest or I'm not going to tell you about it."

"OK, OK!"

"And it's all to do with catching the disease. So when they say 'ring o' roses' – that refers to the pink flush under the skin, and 'pocket full of posies' – they're talking about the preventatives, the dried herbs and stuff that people kept sniffing to try and hold off the disease."

"Right," I said slowly. "What else?"

"When they say 'a-tishoo, a-tishoo' – that's about the sneezing that was one of the first symptoms of plague. And 'all fall down' is them actually dropping down dead."

"OK," I said. "I see all that. But what's it got to do with the field and the wood in Bensbury?"

Jenna shrugged. "I don't know. All I know is . . . at least, all I *feel* is . . . there's something very strange and wrong in that field. Something within that group of trees, probably."

I grinned. "That's good," I said, rubbing my hands. "More ghosts and stuff to investigate."

"Huh," she said. "You didn't say that a couple of weeks ago when we found the skeleton in the trunk – as I remember it you went green and broke the record for the hundred-metre dash to get out of there."

"Rubbish!" I said.

We walked on, and when we reached the gate which led into the field, Jenna paused and screwed up her eyes with concentration.

"Can you hear anything?" I asked after a decent moment. "Any singing?"

She shook her head.

"Come on, then. Let's head towards those trees and see if there's anything else going on."

To be honest, I didn't think there would be anything going on, because who'd ever heard of a haunted field? But I was bored with being at home and having to be polite to a lot of old wrinklies and was willing to go along with anything that had spooky possibilities.

Yeah, I thought that at first, but as we climbed under a line of barbed wire to enter Corpses' Copse, a shiver ran down my back. One moment we were outside in the sunlight, the next we were under a dark canopy of trees and plunged into darkness and silence, and I got a sudden attack of the jitters.

"Where are we going?" I asked, trying to peer around the tree trunks and see through the gloom.

"Dunno. We'll just try and make our way through, I suppose," Jenna said. "See how long it takes us to come out the other side."

We walked on slowly, our eyes gradually getting used to the dim light, our footsteps muffled because the ground was thick with dead, damp leaves. There were fallen twigs and rotting branches all around, but no sign of anything growing or anything green. It was strange, too, how we seemed to be completely cut off from the outside world. There were no birds, no trace of wildlife – not even any sounds of far-off traffic.

"Suppose we get lost in here?" Jenna said suddenly. "Maybe we should be tying string round the trees as we pass – or leaving a trail of breadcrumbs like in *Hansel and Gretel*."

I ignored that remark, treating it with the contempt it deserved. "I wonder why it's called Corpses' Copse," I said instead, getting a sudden, gruesome vision of a row of dead bodies hanging from trees.

"When we get out. . ."

". . .*if* we get out," I corrected in a doom-laden voice.

"We'll go and ask Ratty Ratcliffe about it. She knows everything. She'll know how it got its name."

"OK," I said, "but –" I stopped because Jenna, one step in front of me, had come to a halt so suddenly that I'd banged into her.

"Look!" she gasped.

I looked over her shoulder and gave a yelp of astonishment, because suddenly we'd come to a clearing; a ragged open space between the dense trees. Stranger still, there was an old building made of rough grey stone blocks with a chimney at each end of it and slits for windows set high in its walls.

"It's the wicked witch's cottage!" Jenna said. "See? It *is* like *Hansel and Gretel*."

I ignored *that*, too.

We circled the place slowly, looking for clues as to what it might be.

"Perhaps it's a woodcutter's hut," Jenna said. "Or a gamekeeper's lodge or something."

I shrugged to say that I didn't have the slightest idea, then jumped up to try and look in one of the windows. "We'll have to try and get inside."

Jenna looked at me and bit her lip. "I'm not sure if we should."

Taking no notice of this bit of girliness, I went round to the door, which was stout, wooden and thick with dirt. It had a broken padlock but only one hinge, and was hanging twisted and jammed in the doorway.

"This just needs a bit of a helping hand," I

said, and I ran at the door and shouldered it hard, as if I was tackling someone at rugby.

The padlock snapped off and the door swung there for a moment, then dropped down flat with an almighty crash on to the floor behind.

"There," I said. "That should scare off any ghosts."

Jenna tiptoed up. "Hello!" she called through the open doorway. "Anyone there?"

"Of course there's not!" I said scornfully. "Don't be an eejit."

Inside, it was just one long room with six rusty iron bedsteads in a row down one side. The strange thing was, instead of it being full of rubbish and dirt and spiders, it was tidy and reasonably clean. There were no cobwebs or dust, and the floor didn't have as much as a dead leaf lying on it.

"Someone must come in here regularly to keep it clean," Jenna said as we looked round.

"If they do, I don't know how they get in," I said, "because to my reckoning no one can have come through that door for about a hundred years. It needed someone of my superior strength to hammer it down."

"I don't understand, then."

I watched Jenna closely as she walked from one end of the room to the other and knew almost immediately when she felt something, because I, too, felt a funny prickling at the back of my neck. A shiver ran through me. "You can feel something, can't you?" I said.

"I can hear voices," she said in a whisper. "Very far off. Like they're miles – or years – away."

"Are they singing again?"

She nodded, head on one side. "Ring a Ring o' Roses. . ." she said in a faraway voice. She listened for a moment and then her face cleared and she walked towards one of the beds. "Look at this," Jenna said, and I saw that beside the bedstead, propped up on a low shelf, was a jagged piece of mirror about a metre long. A lot of its silvering had gone and it was dark and spotted with age.

"It's just a bit of mirror," I said.

"No, I think it's more than that," she said in a strange voice. "Or less. . ."

"What're you talking about? What d'you mean?"

"Look – it doesn't show my reflection."

"*What?*"

"I can't see me in it. Instead I can—" She suddenly gave a piercing scream and jumped backwards.

"What's the matter *now*?" I asked, going up behind her and trying to see what it was that she'd seen in there.

"I saw someone *else's* face staring at me!" she said, sounding terrified. "It was another girl. Not me at all."

"Come off it!" I felt I had to say this, even though I knew she wouldn't have made up something like that. "You can't have seen someone else!" I stood between her and the broken mirror, waving my hands at it. "There you are!" I said. "Those are my hands there now. You can see *them* all right, can't you?"

Jenna looked round at me, wide-eyed. "I definitely saw someone, Jake. And her lips moved and she spoke to me. Spoke to me in my head..."

"What did she say?"

"She said, 'In this year of plague, Lord have mercy upon us...'"

CHAPTER THREE

" 'Lord have mercy upon us,' " said Ratty Ratcliffe to us the following day. "That's what the parish had written on people's doors when they were afflicted with plague. There would be a red cross painted on the door as well, and the people inside would be shut up for forty days, until everyone in the house was dead or they were thought to be clear of plague."

"And what about 'Ring a Ring o' Roses'?" Jenna asked.

"Oh yes, it's well known that that nursery rhyme dates from around the time of the great plague." Ratty stared at us, beady eyes gleaming and head on one side like a particularly inquisitive rodent. "My local history society did a most interesting paper on it. But why d'you want to know all this?"

"Well. . ." Jenna said, floundering and nudging me to say something.

"It's a project," I said immediately. That usually satisfied wrinklies.

"It's strange you should be doing a project on the great plague," Ratty said, "because did you know that in the seventeenth century they used part of one of the farm fields as a plague pit?"

My attention, which had started to wander towards next season's fixtures, suddenly focused on Ratty again. "*What?*"

"Which field?" Jenna asked.

"The one near Murray's Farm – the little wood nearby has always been known as Corpses' Copse," Ratty said, causing Jenna and I to gulp and then fall silent. She went on, "In the cities thousands died of plague, and the churchyards became completely full – there was no cremation then, of course. They had to dispose of the bodies somehow, so they put them on carts, brought them out to the countryside and tipped them all into great big pits dug for the purpose."

"How awful," Jenna shuddered.

"Yes, I'm afraid it *was* awful," Ratty said. "They put quicklime over the top to help the bodies to decompose, and then let nature take its course. They do say that to this day, though, crops don't grow in that field. Although I wouldn't know about that, not being a farmer."

"What about the hut?" Jenna blurted out. "The hut in the middle of the copse of trees?"

Ratty did her enquiring rodent look. "I don't know of any hut," she said, "but my history group would be very interested if there was."

"There's definitely—" Jenna began, and I nudged her hard to be quiet.

"We must have heard wrongly," I interrupted. "It was just something someone said to us."

"Well, if you find one, let me know," Ratty said, setting off with her old fogey shopping carrier on wheels (everyone in the village had at least one of these).

"You didn't have to nudge me quite so hard," Jenna said indignantly when Ratty was out of earshot. "I'll probably get a terrible bruise there now."

"Sorry," I said, "but if there's something funny about that place the last thing we want is to have Ratty and the local history society marching through it. We've got to investigate it properly ourselves first."

She poked me back. "OK. But just watch it."

When we went back to the shop, Mum was making up a box of groceries for us to deliver to the vicar's house. We were sitting outside waiting for her to finish this when we spotted Stuffer Starr coming towards us. I had a certain question burning to be asked, so I quickly jumped up and put on my polite and enquiring face.

"Excuse me, Mr Starr," I said. "We're doing a project and we wondered if we could ask you something about your . . . er . . . trade."

"Oh yes?" said Stuffer Starr. He was big and grey and rather furry around the ears and nose, as if his own stuffing was coming loose. "What's that, then?"

I coughed, trying to phrase it properly. "You know taxidermy. . ."

"I should do."

"Well, how big an animal can you stuff?"

"Very big," he said. "Foxes, horses, polar bears. No limit, really."

"And do things have to be *furry* to be stuffed?"

Jenna asked, catching on to what I wanted to know.

He looked puzzled. "What exactly do you mean?"

"Is it only ones with fur and hair, or could you do a *bald* sort of animal?" Jenna asked delicately.

"What?"

I decided to jump in with both feet. "What we mean is, could you do a *person*?"

"Oh, certainly!" Stuffer said. "It would be quite possible – given the right circumstances – for a person to be preserved. Got a candidate you want to put forward, then? Taxidermy is a fine and exclusive art form, you know," he went on proudly, "and it's a craft that's dying out. Not enough people are interested in it these days."

"Well, *we're* very interested, aren't we, Jenna? For our . . . er . . . project."

Jenna nodded enthusiastically. "Oh yes, we're very interested indeed."

"Really?" Stuffer asked, looking well pleased. "If you wait while I do the shopping and help me carry my groceries back, I'll show you some of my stuffed furry friends."

"Great!" Jenna and I said.

"Yuuckk," Jenna shuddered once he'd gone. "Furry friends. I wonder what they died of."

* * *

We waited for Stuffer to come out of the shop with a big cardboard box full of food and I carried it back for him. We passed Mr Adams's house – still no sign of life there – and then Stuffer led us into his own house and showed us into the sitting room.

The first thing we saw was a glass case reaching from the floor to the ceiling filled with all sorts of different birds. These weren't sparrows and pigeons and your ordinary stuff, but birds of all shapes and sizes and with feathers of every colour of the rainbow. Some had their wings spread as if they were flying, some were perched on branches, and some were smaller and placed inside nests, looking out for a bigger bird coming back with a (stuffed) fat worm in its beak.

"Wow!" I said.

Jenna didn't say anything.

Next to this case was what looked like the bottom half of a tree, stuck in a pot and spreading across one whole wall. Along the branches ran a tribe of little creatures: mice, squirrels, moles, ferrets and other things I wasn't quite sure of the names of. They were scooting along the branches or sitting feeding, or just curled up asleep. At the foot of the tree was a fox, sitting on its haunches like a dog, with a gingery-feathered chicken in its mouth.

"What d'you think of them two, eh?" Stuffer said proudly. "Roadkill. Found 'em both on the road, just like that."

"Brilliant!" I said.

"Gross," whispered Jenna, but luckily Stuffer didn't hear her.

There were other stuffed things placed around the room: a sturdy black and white badger, two dogs carrying sticks in their mouths, and a lamb standing just in front of the fireplace. Where other people had sofas and chairs, Stuffer had stoats and hares.

When he'd showed us everything in the room, he told us how long he'd had them and how he'd come by the bodies. Some were roadkill, some – like in the case of the lamb – a farmer had passed on to him, others had been village people's pets, some he said he'd just found dead in hedges and holes. He started to tell us how he killed those that weren't *quite* dead but when I glanced at Jenna she looked as if she was going to be sick so I thought I'd better change the subject. I looked out of the window towards Mr Adams's house.

"Has your neighbour come back yet?" I asked. "Only we've got a registered package waiting for him at the post office."

"No, he hasn't," Stuffer said. "And the longer he stays away the better I'll like it."

"Don't you get on, then?" Jenna asked.

"No, we most certainly don't!" Stuffer pursed his lips and puffed out enough breath to make his nose hair quiver with rage. "Never have done."

"Why's that?" I asked.

"Because he's a snob, that's why. Thinks he's better than anyone else in the village with his airs and graces and his Fancy Dan clothes. Wears a cloak and black top hat, if you please."

"What, all the time?" I asked.

"Even to do his shopping in?" Jenna said incredulously.

"He doesn't know everyone's laughing at him behind his back!" Stuffer went on.

"What else does he do that's so awful?" I asked.

"He plays tricks on me, that's what. And he hides in dark corners of the garden and jumps out at me. Tries to scare me."

"Really?" Jenna asked.

"And he made it rain the day I had a garden party."

"Made it rain. . ." Jenna repeated faintly.

I just grinned. Stuffer hated Mr Adams all right – but did he hate him enough to *stuff* him?

In the hall on our way out we stroked a stuffed tortoiseshell cat which had been placed with a stuffed mouse between its paws. It was outside a door marked "No Entry".

"Have you got more animals in there?" I asked Stuffer.

He pursed his lips. "No one goes in that room," he said. "That's my surgery."

I raised my eyebrows at Jenna as Stuffer walked on to open the front door. "His surgery!" I whispered. "Bet Mr Adams is in there waiting to be stuffed. . ."

We thanked Stuffer and began to walk back home. I would have liked to have hung around a bit longer – I had a fancy to look round the back of Mr Adams's house for clues as to where he might be – but I thought Stuffer might be watching us.

Jenna gave a long drawn-out shudder. "All those poor animals give me the creeps," she said. "Stuffing things shouldn't be allowed."

"What?" I said. "They're great! When I get some money I'm going to commission a great big black bear, and then I'm going to stand it just inside my bedroom door to stop people coming in."

"The state of *your* bedroom!" she said. "Who'd want to go in there anyway?"

In bed that night, though, I was woken up by Jenna coming in and shaking my shoulder. "Wake up, Jake," she said. "Wake up!"

I burrowed further under my duvet, but she sat on the edge of my mattress and bounced it up and down until I opened my eyes. When I did so, she was sitting on my bed with her duvet wrapped around her. She looked a bit strange and pale, but that might just have been because of the moonlight shining through the window.

Groaning, I struggled to sit up. "What is it?" I asked. "Don't tell me you're having nightmares about Stuffer's animals."

"No, it's not that," she said. "I can't sleep. Whenever I close my eyes, I keep hearing the same voice."

"What sort of a voice?"

She pointed out of the window. "It's a voice from out there. From the wood."

"You daft head – that's nearly a kilometre

away! Even if there was a voice you couldn't have heard it from that distance."

"I did hear it!" she said emphatically. "And it was definitely from Corpses' Copse."

"Well, what did it say?"

"It was the voice of that girl in the mirror. She was calling to me and she sounded so sad and mournful."

"Blimey," I muttered.

"She was calling my name. '*Jenna, Jenna. Please!*' she kept saying. She wants me to go and help her!" Jenna looked at me, chewing her bottom lip. "Will you come with me?"

"*What?*" I said. "Go out to the woods in the middle of the night? Get real."

"She really needs me, though!"

"Too bad."

"Will you come with me tomorrow, then?"

I sighed. "Look," I said, "if she's been there ever since the seventeenth century, then she can hang on a bit longer."

"But we ought to go there as quickly as we can!"

I thought – in the interests of getting back to sleep – that it was best to humour her. "Yeah, yeah. Tomorrow," I said, falling back on my bed. "Or sometime soon."

"Do you really think she is from those times? Like a time slip thing?"

"Dunno," I said, trying to pull up the duvet so I could disappear under it. "I mean, it's all a bit crazy, isn't it? The girl in the mirror thing sounds about as likely as Mr Adams being stuffed by Stuffer Starr."

"But in this place," she said, "who knows?"

"You're right," I said, yawning hugely. "But clear off now and we'll talk about it tomorrow."

CHAPTER FOUR

Of course, it all looked different in the morning.

"I can hardly remember the voice now," Jenna said as we poured breakfast cereal down our throats. "I suppose it just could have been some sort of nightmare brought on by seeing all those dead animals. I do want to go back to that hut sometime, though. Even if it's just to try and prove to myself that I didn't see anyone in the mirror."

I rammed in another mouthful. "In the meantime," I said, "we have to investigate the strange disappearance of Mr Adams."

"Mr Adams?" Mum asked, coming through from the shop just at that moment. "Is he back yet?"

"Not sure," I said. "D'you want us to take that packet over to his house again?"

"If you wouldn't mind." Mum looked at me suspiciously. "Funny how you're so keen to help me all of a sudden."

"He just sounds . . . interesting."

"They say he wears a long cloak and black top hat," Jenna added.

"Don't be silly!" said Mum.

After breakfast she got his registered packet and the form he was supposed to sign to say he'd received it, and handed them over with instructions to bring them straight back if he wasn't there. As we walked across the green I felt the packet, shook it a bit, tried to work out what was inside. It was about as long as my hand, and squarish, and done up in corrugated cardboard and black tape. I examined the ends of the packet closely, wondering if they might accidentally come open, but unfortunately they seemed to be stuck down hard.

We knocked on Mr Adams's door. There was no reply, but then we didn't think there would be. We knocked again and then I flipped up the latch of the side gate which led into his garden.

"I think we ought to knock on his back door,

in case he's in but he can't hear us at the front," I said to Jenna. "Then we can look in his kitchen window," I added in a whisper.

"What are you two doing?" The high-pitched squeal drifted over from Squeaker's garden, and when we looked round she was standing at her kitchen door wearing a flowery dress and big furry slippers with pom-poms on.

"We're just trying to deliver Mr Adams's post," I said, hammering at his back door.

"He's not there!" Squeaker said. "You know he's not there."

"All the same, we have to check," I said smoothly.

"The Royal Mail must get through," Jenna added.

We knocked a couple more times, and all the while Squeaker was standing there staring at us suspiciously.

"And I thought *I* was nosey," Jenna said under her breath.

"I think we ought to look through his windows," I said to Jenna, loud enough for Squeaker to hear. "Just in case he's ill or anything."

"He's not there, I tell you!" Squeaker said,

exasperated. "I'd have known if he'd been taken ill."

Taking no notice of this, we peered through Mr Adams's window.

We were glad we did, because what we saw there was very odd indeed. The table was set up for a meal, with salt, pepper and tomato ketchup bottle in the middle. The food, though (sausages and chips), was still actually on the plate, half eaten. A knife and fork rested on the plate's edge and there was a folded newspaper to one side, with a pair of glasses on top of this. Mr Adams had disappeared right in the middle of his nosh!

"Taken off by aliens – what d'you reckon?" I said to Jenna.

"It's like that ship we did at school," she exclaimed.

"The *Marie Celeste*."

She nodded. "They found it just floating around on its own. The crew had just disappeared in the middle of whatever they were doing, and they never *ever* found out what happened to them."

"So weird!" I said, casting my eyes around Mr Adams's kitchen for any other clues (which included squinting down to the floor to make sure he wasn't just lying there, stone dead).

"Satisfied yourselves?" Squeaker called. "Believe me that he's not there now, do you?"

"Yes, thank you very much," I said, ultra-politely.

"Expect we'll check again next week, though," Jenna said.

"Squeak to you soon!" I added.

We went out of the gate, closing it carefully behind us, and walked back past Stuffer's house. It was then, glancing into his back garden, that I had a shock.

"I don't believe it!" I said to Jenna. "Take a look through to Stuffer's back garden – at what's standing guard over his runner beans."

She looked and gave a scream.

"But try not to draw attention to it," I said, a bit too late.

"Is it. . . Is it Mr Adams?" she stuttered.

I nodded. "It certainly looks like it could be."

In front of us was a scarecrow. But a tall, very human and horrid-looking scarecrow, wearing a long tatty black cloak with a top hat pulled down over its face.

For a moment or two we just stood there,

transfixed, then Jenna said, "It can't be! Stuffer wouldn't really. . ."

"He might," I said. "If he was pushed."

Because from where we were standing, the scarecrow looked mighty real. . .

"We need to get in Stuffer's garden and examine that scarecrow," I said as we walked back to the shop. "We know he *can* stuff people, now we've got to find out if he *has*."

Jenna shook her head. "You can't really expect me to believe that he's killed Mr Adams, then stuffed him and stood him in his garden for everyone to see."

"Anything's possible round here," I said with a shrug. "Remember, we're not dealing with ordinary people. We're dealing with the seriously weird: the Bensbury Batties."

Mum gave us a look as we came through the shop door. "You two look thick as thieves," she said. "What are you plotting?"

"Nothing," I said innocently. "We were just talking about Mr Starr's garden. It's full of really interesting things."

"Really?" Mum asked disbelievingly.

"Yes. The . . . er . . . vegetables and runner

beans. I was thinking of asking him how he makes them."

"How he *makes* them, Jake?" Mum shook her head. "Oh yes, I can tell you're really interested. Don't you mean how he *grows* them?"

"Whatever," I said.

She looked at us and frowned. "I don't want you finding any more skeletons in trunks," she said. "You just keep yourselves to yourselves." She came out from behind the post office counter. "Now, since you're both here, I'll leave you in charge while I pop out the back for a cuppa. Call me if you need me."

Over the next half-hour we served three customers. Mrs Huge-o came by for some packets of custard creams, Grouchy Green wanted a jar of pickles and looked through about forty jars to find the one which had the biggest onions, and Snotty Snape wanted a box of tissues.

By subtle questioning we managed to find out the following things:

1. That Mr Adams was not only weird, but also the village show-off, always full of himself – what he'd done and where he'd been.

2. That Stuffer went out at night looking for dead animals to stuff, and nothing was safe in his hands. He would "stuff a fly if he could catch one", Mrs Huge-o told us.
3. That he and Stuffer had fallen out because they'd both taken a fancy to their mutual neighbour, Squeaker Squires.

"Mr Adams and Stuffer fell out over Squeaker?" Jenna said incredulously when we heard that.

"Shopping carriers on wheels at forty paces!" I added.

The only thing we couldn't get more information about was Corpses' Copse, because although everyone had heard of it, and told us it wasn't a good place to go, they didn't seem to know why no one ever went there, or why crops didn't grow around it. Snotty Snape said that as a girl she wasn't allowed to play there, although she never knew why.

I stared at her, trying to imagine her "as a girl" and failing miserably, seeing as she was now about a hundred and ten. True to her name, she had a drop on the end of her nose which quivered gently as she spoke.

"And did you ever hear anything about an old hut in that wood?" Jenna asked her.

Snotty shook her head for such a long time that I was afraid the drop might fall off. "There's no hut there," she said. "I'd have heard. People would have talked about it."

"But we've—" Jenna began – and luckily was interrupted by Mum coming through from the back. "What hut are you talking about?" she said. "You mentioned the wood but you didn't mention any hut. I don't want you going into those sorts of places – they're hideouts for tramps and rough-sleepers. And the roof will probably fall in on you as well."

"But I don't think there is a hut!" Snotty said.

Mum looked at her, and then at me and Jenna closely, then let the subject drop. Smiling at Snotty she said, "I'm so sorry they've been holding you up with all their questions, Mrs Snape," she said. "Is there anything else I can get you?"

Snotty said there was nothing at all, so the giant-sized box of tissues was put into her trolley, I opened the door for her and off she went.

"What about that drip on her nose!" I said as she left. "Did it actually fall off?"

Mum tutted. "You mustn't bother our customers with so many questions," she said. "Talk about giving them a grilling – I was quite expecting to find them sitting down in here with a white light shining in their faces."

"We were just asking them about life in the country," I said innocently.

"Only being polite," Jenna put in.

"Thought you'd like that," I continued.

Mum frowned. "And what *is* all this about Mr Adams? Why are you so interested in him all of a sudden?"

I shrugged. "We just... We've just been wondering why he's disappeared."

"Hmm..." she said. "I know you two well enough to know there's something else." After a moment she added, "Anyway, about this hut. I don't want you going inside it."

"You heard Snotty..."

"Jake!"

"Mrs Snape, I mean. She said there's no hut there, so how could we go in it?"

"Hmm..." Mum said again, not sounding convinced.

As she went behind the post office counter, Jenna looked at me. "What's going on?" she said in a low voice. "Is there a hut there or not? We couldn't have just imagined it, could we?"

I shrugged. "We'd better go back tomorrow and find out."

CHAPTER FIVE

"We must be mad," I said to Jenna. "I can't believe we're traipsing about in the pouring rain."

She glanced up. "It's not raining so much under these trees."

"No, but it's pretty grim." I looked up, pulling a face. It was damp, dark and gloomy in Corpses' Copse, and more like November than July.

I'd felt totally fed up that morning, hadn't wanted to come out, just felt like staying in bed and sulking. I'd been thinking about where we used to live, what a laugh I'd had, how great it had been to get up on a Saturday morning, call on my mates and go and kick a ball about in the park or go out on skateboards. Here? Here there was nothing to do, nowhere to do it and I didn't have any mates. I really needed to get myself a life. . .

"I dunno if I can be bothered to do this," I grumbled as I scuffed my way along.

Jenna turned on me. "Stop moaning! Yesterday you wanted to come here. It was your idea! And anyway, what else is there to do?"

"That's just it. Nothing!"

"Well, then." A trickle of rain ran down her face. "Besides, this was going to be our hobby while we were living here. We were going to be ghost-hunters."

"Yeah, yeah. Whatever." I looked at her. "You're turning into Snotty Snape – you've got a great big drip on the end of your nose."

She brushed it off with her sleeve and we walked on, with Jenna leading the way. I don't always let her go first, but – as when we'd come here before – she seemed to know which direction to go in. I certainly didn't.

"How come you know where this hut is when all the trees look the same?" I asked.

"Dunno," she said. After a moment she added, "Funny, that. Something seems to be pulling me along so I know the way without thinking about it. And sometimes. . ."

"What?"

"Sometimes I can hear that girl's voice in my head, quite clearly. 'Come on, Jenna' she's saying. 'Come and find me'."

"Crumbs," I said. We walked on, me feeling quite pleased that I wasn't psychic. I didn't want to hear any voices . . . or rather I did – but only if they were saying "Great goal, Jake, my old mate!"

I was about to say that we must have lost our way when we came upon the clearing and there was the hut in all its coldness and bleakness, the rain lashing down on to its slate roof and running in streams down the grey stone walls. It looked about as inviting as a muddy pitch in a snowstorm.

"Here we are," I said. "Cosy cottage. We'd better make a dash for it."

I pulled my hoody further over my head and prepared to run out of the shelter of the trees and across the clearing. As I took a step forward, though, my foot caught on something and I nearly fell head first in the mud. When I looked down I saw what looked like a long plank of rough wood sticking out of the sodden leaves and bracken.

"Hang on!" I said to Jenna, and I bent down

and pulled it out, getting a splinter under my thumbnail in the process.

"It's like a sign. It's got words on it," she said.

We laid it flat on the ground and kicked all the leaves and gunge off. We could just about see letters then, carved into the surface. They read:

PEST HOUSE. KEEP AWAY!

"Pest house!" Jenna said. "You know what *that* is, don't you?"

"Course I do. Pest is pestilence. Another word for plague."

"So – I get it now – this little place was some sort of isolation hospital."

"It's still got the beds!"

"I bet it belonged to the village, and people with the plague were made to come and live out here until they got better. . ."

"Or until they died."

We stared at the sign. "We ought to take that back to the village sometime," I said. "They might like it for the village hall. Or Ratty's history society."

"OK. We will," Jenna said. She glanced

towards the hut. "But let's go and investigate the hut now. That girl's waiting. . ."

We ran across to the doorway of the hut – and it was here that I got a bit of a shock, for although I'd shouldered the door down flat when we'd come before, *now* it was back in place, big and dirty and spattered with rain.

"*Whaaa?*" I said in shock.

"Someone's put it back up!" said Jenna.

I stared at the door, truly puzzled. When I'd bashed it down before, its rusty padlock had gone flying in at least two different directions. Now the door was standing once more with the padlock back in position. It was as if we'd never been there, never touched it at all.

What was going on?

"I suppose I'll just have to knock it down again," I said, and I took a deep breath, smashed into the door and shouldered it. As before, the lock broke and dropped in pieces to the ground.

I pushed one bit deep into the wet earth with my foot. "OK," I said. "There is *no* way that that padlock could be put back together. If it is, then. . ."

But Jenna wasn't listening, she was moving past me to get inside.

I followed her into the hut. It was exactly the same as before, very gloomy because of the weather, but looking neat and clean. There were a couple of puddles about and water was dripping into them from holes in the roof.

"We should have brought our torches," I said.

Jenna didn't reply to this, just stood looking about her, hugging her arms around herself. "There's an awful lot of pain here. Pain and misery."

I didn't say anything. It spooked me when she said things like that.

"People died in this room," she went on. "They arrived here and they never went home again." She stared around the room, shivering. "I can almost see them, Jake! It was crowded and smelly. There were two or three people in every bed, and others lying on the floor with old bits of material over them, and everyone was crying or calling out, or just lying there too weak to speak, just waiting to die."

"No bundle of laughs, then?" I said, making a feeble attempt to lighten things up.

She ignored me. "There was no medicine," she continued, "and some days there wasn't even any food. They just relied on people coming by and giving them scraps that their animals left."

"OK," I said, "I feel sorry for them and everything but that's all in the past now. What about your pal in the mirror? It was her you really came to find out about."

She bit her lip, looking at me. "I feel a bit scared. Will you come and look with me?"

"OK," I said carelessly, and I began whistling a football anthem under my breath, just to show that I wasn't frit.

When we reached the broken mirror Jenna stood right in front of it and fell silent. Although it was dark, I could definitely see her reflection.

"I can see you!" I said cheerfully. "There you are standing in. . ."

"Just be quiet for a minute, Jake. I need to concentrate. And I have to . . . to *commune*."

"Get you!" I said under my breath. But I did stop talking.

A moment later she said, "Look, Jake . . . the mirror. My reflection is dissolving!"

"*What?*"

"It's going all misty around the edges . . . fading into someone else's face. Can't you see?"

I stared into the mirror over her shoulder, screwed up my eyes and concentrated really hard.

I thought I *might* have seen something . . . Jenna's face turning into someone else's . . . growing harder and thinner, her eyes glittering. . . But then I could have been mistaken.

"Hello. . ." Jenna whispered, staring at the mirror. "It's you, isn't it?"

"Jenna, can you really . . . *really* see someone?" I asked hoarsely. "What's she doing? Is it that same girl?"

"Yes. The same," Jenna said in a low, spellbound voice.

"Ask her what her name is."

Someone answered me – and I swear the voice didn't come from Jenna. "Sorrel," the voice said. "My name is Sorrel Larkin."

I repeated it, and Jenna glanced round at me. "You heard her as well?"

I shook my head. "You heard her. And I heard her through you."

Jenna turned back to the mirror. "I can see her more clearly this time. She's wearing a brown linen dress, and a grubby old apron. Her hair is a gingery colour, curly, and she's got a little white cap on her head."

I couldn't see any of this, however much I squished up my eyes. It had grown so dim in the mirror that I couldn't really see anything at all. "Ask her what she wants," I said.

Jenna nodded, took a deep breath. "Sorrel," she addressed the mirror, "we'll help you if we can. What is it that you want?"

There was a strange noise, faraway, blobby and echoing, which I can only describe as like someone trying to speak underwater. And then I heard, more clearly, someone cry, "I want to be saved! I want to come out of this mirror!"

Jenna and I both jumped at this, but before we could do anything there was a sudden vast flash of lightning which lit up the whole place in a hard white light, followed almost immediately by a tremendous clap of thunder, the loudest I've ever heard. Jenna screamed – I think I probably yelled – and then I grabbed her arm and we both ran out of that hut like we were Wayne Rooney slicing through an opposition's defence.

We were so shocked that we ran almost all the way home – not stopping to look back.

CHAPTER SIX

"So what do you *really* think it was?" Jenna asked the next morning. She was sitting on the green while I carefully dribbled my football around the *No Ball Games* notice.

"It was thunder and lightning," I said.

"No, I mean – was it real, ordinary thunder and lightning, or something *other*? Some sort of warning?"

"What, you mean like a thunderclap of doom?" I asked, grinning.

"Be serious, Jake. This is important. Which was it?"

"Dunno," I said, which was less than helpful, but all I could say about it. This ghost-hunting lark was pretty new and I didn't know what the rules were. Football – well, you knew where you were with football, everything was set down in writing and you had a ref to sort out any tricky bits. You could have asked me anything you liked about football and I could have answered it. Ghosts, though? Ghosts were a different ball game altogether.

"We'll have to go back there," Jenna said.

"Right." I paused. "You're joking, of course."

She shook her head at me. "No, I mean it."

"What good would that do?" I asked scornfully.

"I need to go back to try and settle things. I won't feel right until I do."

I groaned. If she went, obviously I'd have to go with her. "Look, there might have been someone there once but they're dead now and—"

"Young man!" a voice called across the green. "Jack, or whatever your name is!"

"Jake," I said, turning. It was Grouchy Green, trundling his shopping trolley along the lane towards our shop.

"Can't you read, boy? You're not supposed to play ball games on the green."

"I'm not actually playing a game," I replied. I'd been thinking about this one for some time and I reckoned I'd got it sorted. "Because playing a game would mean you had an opponent," I explained, "and I haven't. What I'm actually doing is just moving the ball around a bit on my own."

He frowned so deeply that a wavy set of railway lines appeared on his forehead. "Impudence!" he said, disappearing into our shop.

I was still moving the ball around and Jenna was still going on about the hut when Stuffer Starr trundled up with *his* trolley and I got an idea for something that would distract her.

"We still need to find out about old Stuffer's scarecrow, don't we?" I said. "So while he's safely inside the shop, let's go along to his garden and investigate a bit; try and find out exactly *what's* in his back garden looking after his lettuces."

"OK," she said, "but it won't take two of us, will it? What about if I hang around here until he comes out, and then delay him by asking him questions, stuffing-animals sorts of questions, while you do the investigating?"

I nodded. "It's a deal," I said. "Try and keep him talking. . ."

Giving my ball a hefty kick across the green, I set off for Stuffer's house. His vegetable patch, where the scarecrow stood with its black cloak blowing about it, was separated from his front garden by a low fence. There was no gate – probably he got into the back garden by going out of his kitchen door – so I'd have to get over that fence. And I ought to have some excuse ready, just in case.

I grinned to myself; knowing what the excuse was going to be. Occasionally being a footballer came in handy. I mean, what was more innocent than claiming that you'd just gone into someone's garden to get your ball back?

I lined the ball up as for a penalty kick, eyeballed the neighbouring opposition (although Squeaker was nowhere to be seen) then took a run and kicked it with deadly accuracy. Like a dream golden goal it travelled across Stuffer's front garden, over the low fence, into the vegetable patch – and took off the head of the scarecrow!

I gulped a bit and began hoping that I hadn't beheaded a real, stuffed person, because if I had it could be messy. . .

I climbed over the low fence adjoining the front

and back gardens and approached the figure cautiously. Was it just a scarecrow – or was it Mr Adams, stuffed to perfection?

Once I was closer I could see straight away (and rather disappointingly) that it wasn't a real person, stuffed or otherwise. It was dead clever, though: its body was made from an old sack filled with crumpled newspaper and its arms were branches with twiggy fingers which protruded from its jacket. The top hat was of black-painted cardboard, the cloak was a plastic binliner and its actual head – now rolling on the ground near the carrots – was a great big round swede. It was a pretty good scarecrow and it was probably meant to look like Mr Adams – but it wasn't him. And I didn't know whether I was pleased about that or not.

"Jake!" Jenna's voice came from behind me and I whipped round.

"Stuffer's coming!" she said. "I kept him there as long as I could." She looked back across the green. "He's just met Horseface Hall, but he could be here in a couple of minutes. What have you found out?"

"It's not Mr Adams. It's meant to look like him, but it's not actually him."

"Thank goodness for that!"

"Mmm. . ." I said.

She glanced across the green again. "You'd better come out of his garden."

"Hang on," I said, and I picked up the swede-head and put it back on the body, then rescued the cardboard top hat and fixed it on top as best I could. I took a few steps into the vegetable patch to retrieve my football, and it was then that a voice said, "Thank you so much. I really don't like being without my head."

I've never fainted, but I nearly did then, because *the voice came from the scarecrow*.

I heard a gasp of shock from Jenna. "How did you do that voice, Jake? You didn't move your lips at all."

"It wasn't me! I . . . I didn't say anything," I said, backing off from the scarecrow fast.

"Going already?" it said. "I so seldom have anyone interesting to talk to. Mr Starr is dull beyond words."

I looked all round, down the garden, past the rows of runner beans and other stuff, but there was no one in sight.

"He's made a pretty poor job of me, too," the scarecrow went on, "considering that the real Mr

Adams cuts such a dashing figure in real life."

"Well, if it's not you speaking," Jenna asked in confusion, "who is it?"

"I don't know!" I yelped. I grabbed my ball, broke into a run and cleared the garden fence faster than a horse in the Grand National.

Just then, from around the corner of the house next door – Squeaker's house – came a tall man with black, slicked-back hair and a dark suit.

He gave a short bow. "I said, are you going already?"

Jenna and I both looked from the scarecrow to the man and back again. "It was you speaking!" I said.

"You threw your voice," Jenna stammered. "Like a ventriloquist."

"Right both times," he said. He smiled and showed very large front teeth. Like tombstones, they were. And his eyes were jet black with – I swear – red rims like a vampire.

Everything suddenly fell into place. "You're Mr Adams!" I said.

"And whom do I have the pleasure of addressing?"

"We're Jake and Jenna," I said. "Our mum runs the shop and post office."

"Ah, yes," he said, coming closer. "The twins. I've just been taking tea with Mrs Squires and she told me that you've been round several times with a package for me."

"We'll bring it tomorrow. . ." I began.

"But what's this? What does your sister keep in her hair?" He reached out to Jenna, took something from behind her ear, bowed and gave her a boiled egg.

"And what are you hiding behind your back, young man?"

He reached behind me, made a flicking movement with his hand, and fanned out a full deck of cards. "Choose a card. Any card."

"You. . . You're a magician!" Jenna said.

"No, my dear," he said. "I am *the* magician. They call me Mr Magic."

I gawped at him a bit. "No one told us *that*." They'd told us about tricks he'd played, and they'd told us that he wore a top hat and cloak, but they hadn't told us he was a *magician*.

He stared at me with his red-rimmed eyes. I tell you, they made me shiver, those eyes. "Mrs Squires says you've been looking through my window."

"We were . . . er . . . just trying to deliver the package."

"When we looked in, though, it seemed like you'd been spirited away in the middle of a meal," Jenna said.

"Ah," said Mr Adams. "It's a ploy of mine, in case a burglar should chance by and look in. If he did, then he'd merely think I was in another room. Clever, don't you think? And just another example of Mr Magic's uncanny foresight."

"But where have you been?" Jenna asked.

He smiled and bared his teeth. "Well, kiddies," he said (which was enough to finish him in my book), "I've been on a cruise. I was the cabaret and the chief entertainment and I was absolutely excellent." He came closer. "Now, if you give me your wristwatch I'll smash it with a hammer and then completely restore it. Or would either of you care to enter my magic disappearing cabinet and never be seen again?"

Jenna glanced at me nervously.

"Can't stop," I said. "We've got to get back."

"Our mum's expecting us!" said Jenna.

"But I love performing to children!" he said. "They believe everything."

"Yeah. Great. Another time." I picked up my ball and Jenna and I began to walk, very quickly, back to the shop.

"Talk about creepy," Jenna said as soon as we were out of earshot.

"Those teeth!"

"All the better to eat you with," Jenna said, shuddering.

"And those eyes of his. . ."

". . .see right through you."

We passed Stuffer coming back towards his house. "Mr Adams is back," I said.

Stuffer groaned. "That's all I need. His white rabbits will be eating my cabbages, his doves will be pooing on my head – and he'll be in the middle of it all, doing his bloody tricks and thinking he's God's gift to the world of entertainment."

"Mr Magic!" Jenna said as we walked on.

"Mr Tragic, more like," I said, and we both sniggered.

So Stuffer hadn't stuffed Mr Adams and made him into a scarecrow . . . but the more we saw of him later the more we wished he *had*. As for the hut in the woods – well, for a couple of days Jenna didn't say much about it and I was hoping that she'd forgotten it. I was busy, anyway, because when I'd been noseying about the village a bit, I'd found a biggish patch of grass up near the new houses in Meadow Lane and I'd started going up there to kick my ball about. To my horror, though, on the third day an old woman came out of one of the nearby houses and said that she'd give me a bit of a kickabout seeing as I had no one to play with. As I stood there, appalled, she brought out a pair of trainers and started lacing them up, so I had to fake an immediate ankle injury and limp away. As if! Imagine if my old mates had seen me.

As I walked down from Meadow Lane and rounded the corner by the church, *something* – I don't know what – made me change my mind about going straight home. Instead I lifted the latch on the iron gate into the churchyard and dribbled my ball through the gravestones which led towards the church. I pushed open the porch door – and there was Jenna, talking to a vicar.

"We were just talking about you," Jenna said, "and then you turned up."

The vicar peered at me over wire-rimmed glasses. "Remarkable," he said. "I've heard about the links between twins before. You two must be very close."

I scowled deeply. "We're not close at all," I

said. "She hates football. I just happened to be having a kickabout up the road, and then I just happened to be coming back and then I just. . ." My voice trailed away. Why *had* I gone in there?

The vicar held out his hand and smiled. He was dressed in a long black vicar's frock thing and the top of his head was completely bald apart from three or four strands of hair combed across his scalp. "You're Jake, of course. Pleased to meet you, young man."

I'd never shaken hands with a vicar before and didn't know what to call him. Your reverence? Sire? Father? Your vicarage? In the end I mumbled something which could have been any of these, then turned to make a face at Jenna. "What're you doing here?" I asked. What are you doing talking to *him*, I wanted to say. Vicars made me feel on edge. Didn't you always have to be careful what you said to them, and never swear or anything?

"I came looking for gravestones," she said. "Gravestones from the time of the plague. I thought I might find Sorrel's grave and find out what happened to her."

"And did you find any?"

She shook her head and the vicar said, "I was

just telling your sister that it all happened much too long ago, I'm afraid. Unless tombstones are of the absolute top quality, they just perish and crumble away. We're talking about nearly three hundred and fifty years, remember."

"So there wouldn't be anything left at all?" I asked.

"Well, even if a memorial stone remained, it's not likely that an inscription would survive," he said. "It would have been out in the grave-yard in all weathers. Besides, in those days only a very few people – the Lord of the Manor, say – would have been rich enough to have a proper stone. Most of the village people would have had just a simple wooden cross, or maybe not even that."

"But didn't everyone just get bunged in the plague pit when they died?" I asked.

He shook his head. "The pit was for the cartloads of dead who came from the city. The villagers would have been buried around their own parish church." He looked at Jenna. "But why all this interest in the plague?"

"Well," Jenna said tentatively, "we're doing a project on it, and we think there was a pest house somewhere near here."

He nodded. "I've heard that rumour, but I've never found any proof. If there had been one, though, it would have disappeared years ago." He smoothed the three strands of hair over his bald patch. "And how did you come across the name Sorrel? Sorrel Larkin, I think you said."

"It's just a name someone gave us," I cut in, in case Jenna had the urge to tell him everything. "We don't know if there really *was* such a person."

"Well, if you want to find out if this person existed, I can let you have copies of the baptism records," the vicar said. "And if it's deaths you're after, I can probably find the relevant Bills of Mortality."

"What are those?" I asked.

"Well, every week the parish would publish a notice showing how many people had died and of what cause. It was mostly so they could check whether the number of people who had the plague was increasing or decreasing," he explained.

"That would be great," Jenna said.

"I can give you the baptism records now, but I'll have to apply to the church archivist – he's the one who keeps the old paperwork in order – for copies of the Bills of Mortality. Give me a few days and I'll get back to you."

We went into his vestry and he found us copies of the baptisms – we had no idea how old Sorrel was but we knew she couldn't be too much older than us so we took records of all babies baptized there in the fifteen years before 1665 – then he showed us to the door.

We thanked him and made our way down the path and out of the side gate, and as I clanged the gate shut behind us he shouted in a very un-vicarlike way, "And with his trusty right foot he drives a mighty pass into the path of young Jake!" and my ball came hurtling over the churchyard to land in the lane beside me.

"Great ball!" I said admiringly as I trapped it. "Decent bloke, that vicar."

CHAPTER SEVEN

"Sorrel!" Jenna suddenly yelled, her finger stabbing at one of the pieces of paper on the floor in front of us. "I've found her! She's really here!"

"Show me," I said a bit grumpily, because she'd found her and I hadn't.

We'd spent the afternoon going through the lists of parish baptisms and it hadn't been easy. The pages were difficult to read because most of them were blotched and stained and the photocopies weren't that good. Whoever had written them couldn't spell, either: I'd seen four different spellings of the name Thomas. There were loads of them, too – talk about breeding like rabbits. Some families had had babies christened every single year, regular as clockwork.

I'd found someone called Patience Larkin born in 1660, but we'd more or less given up on Sorrel.

Jenna held the page out towards me, her hand shaking a bit.

"Sorrel Larkin," she read out. "Baptized on September tenth in 1555. She's only about ten or eleven then, poor little thing!"

"*Was* only about ten or eleven," I corrected.

"Her mother was called Ellen, and her father was James. He was a wheelwright."

I studied the page she was holding up. "OK, she existed once. But it doesn't prove that she actually comes through time, to that mirror in that hut. . ."

"How else could I have got the name?" Jenna said. "Sorrel Larkin – she told me her name as clearly as anything. I couldn't just have made it up."

"Maybe it's just a coincidence," I said. "You saw the name written somewhere and remembered it. . ."

"Rubbish!" Jenna said.

I shrugged. Yeah, it was rubbish. And now that Jenna had proof that the girl had really existed, she wasn't going to let things rest. . .

* * *

"Watch out!" Jenna said as we were hanging around outside the shop later that afternoon. "Mr Tragic approaching across the green from the right."

I groaned. Mr Tragic was living up to his name all right. He'd come in the shop the day before and produced a tap which he'd stuck on my head and turned on (it had been this trick, apparently, which had been in the registered package). The day before that he'd brought a basket into the shop and when Mum had opened the lid to put in his shopping two doves had flown out, and on Saturday he'd insisted on removing ping-pong balls from the noses of all our customers.

As if this wasn't bad enough he always wore the full magician's gear (black cloak lined with red silk, shiny top hat and white gloves) and after each trick he'd smile in a narrow, patronizing way and say, "You have been fooled again by Mr Magic!"

We could see why everyone hated him.

"Let's cut, then!" I said swiftly. "Where shall we go?"

"Corpses' Copse!"

I groaned, but what with Mr Tragic bearing down on us, couldn't think of a good enough excuse. Besides, the sun was shining, birds were twittering and it didn't seem possible that we'd gone all mental just because we'd heard a clap of thunder. We'd go to the hut now, I decided, Jenna could speak to the girl (if there really was a girl there) and tell her sorry, but unfortunately there was no way she was going to get out of the mirror so she'd have to stay put. And then this girl would go away and be out of Jenna's head and we could get on with investigating another spooky mystery – we'd already heard a customer in the shop say that they reckoned they had a ghost in their shed.

I quickly parked my football outside the shop and we went off in the opposite direction to Mr Tragic, ignoring his cry of, "Kiddies! Come back! I've got a new trick to show you!"

As we walked through the wood towards the hut it carried on being sunny and we even saw a couple of rabbits, so it wasn't until we actually reached the pest house that I began to feel the slightest bit spooked. And then I did feel *very* spooked, because the old front door was back in position and covered in dirt and cobwebs, the whole padlock was hanging there again, and the place showed no sign of having been disturbed for years and years.

"What keeps happening here?" I said, staring at the door in bafflement. "Who puts it all back each time?"

Jenna was staring at it. "I don't think anyone does," she said in a low voice.

"What d'you mean? You've seen me knock this door down twice before – now it's up again!"

"I think," she said, "that each time we come to this place, we're coming back to exactly the same time."

"Eh? What d'you mean?" I didn't know what she was talking about. If I'd been in a cartoon I would have been standing there with a big question mark above my head.

"Look, I think we're coming back to one particular time on one particular day," she explained. "So no matter what we do when we come here or what changes we make, when we come back again it's always, say..." she shrugged, "...two o'clock on the afternoon of twelfth October 1665 or whatever."

"Oh wow," I said. "I see." I frowned at her.

"But how d'you know that?"

She shrugged. "I don't know how. I just do."

"Hmm," I said, considering the situation. Maybe I'd try out Jenna's theory by leaving something behind in the hut this time, something modern: a sweet wrapper or a piece of chewing gum. If she was right, then it would have disappeared by the time we came back again.

If we ever came back.

Jenna suddenly shivered, although it was as warm as anything standing there in the bright sunshine. "Shall we go in?" she asked. "Want to do your macho bit?"

"OK," I said, trying to sound unconcerned. I swaggered forward, flexed my muscles and shouldered the door down.

We went inside the little building and stood looking round us. It was just as dim and dreary as it had been before, the sun outside making no impression on the place at all apart from casting one shaft of sunlight, thick with dust, through a high window. I began whistling in a jolly sort of way to combat the weird feeling that was creeping over me. It wasn't exactly dread, nor fear – more the sort of sinking feeling you get when you realize your team just hasn't got what it takes to reach the season's play-offs. Something was going to happen. And I didn't think it was going to be good.

"So what are we actually here for?" I asked, leaving off whistling for a moment.

"I'm not sure yet," Jenna said. She had her eyes on the mirror and was slowly going closer. "I just want to see if there's anything I can do for her. For Sorrel. And I mean – we're supposed to be ghost-hunters, aren't we? Well, this is what ghost-hunters do."

She was standing in front of the slice of mirror now. I began whistling again.

"For God's sake, stop!" she said. "Or at least whistle in tune."

"Oh, pardon me for breathing," I said.

"How am I supposed to be psychic and reach Sorrel's spirit when you're whistling some old football song or other?"

"Reaching Sorrel's spirit, eh?" I couldn't resist saying, but she didn't look at me, didn't even seem to hear me, she was so intent on gazing into that mirror.

"Sorrel. . ." she called softly.

"Is she there?"

Jenna turned on me. "*Ssshh!*"

"Sorrel..." she called again, and then said, "Oh, there you are!"

I jumped, but thought I'd get my head bitten off if I asked anything, so I just peered over Jenna's shoulder into the mirror to see what I could see. The answer was: nothing. No reflection at all. Not of me or Jenna or anything else, just a dusty blackness.

Jenna carried on staring at this nothing. "What can I do to help you?" she asked, and I heard a strange whispering and gurgling that somehow said, "*I want to come through...*"

I shivered all over. "What did she say?" I asked. Just for confirmation.

Jenna turned to me, her eyes shining. "She wants to come through."

"What's that supposed to mean?"

"She wants to come into our time," Jenna said. "And she needs me to help her." She put a hand towards the mirror and I heard some other words kind of vibrating through Jenna, but couldn't make them out clearly until Jenna translated.

"Sorrel says she'll die if she's left here in the pest house!" she said. "She says her mother and father are dead already, and her two younger sisters have the plague marks on them and are likely to die at any moment."

"Yes, but. . ." The whole thing was amazing – not to mention unbelievable. "I'm sorry for her and all that, but it's nothing to do with us, is it? And whatever's going to happen to her has already happened! She's the seventeenth century and we're the twenty-first. We can't change that."

"We can!" Jenna said with a mad sort of urgency to her voice. "We can stop it happening to her, stop her dying! This mirror is like a window into the seventeenth century. We could bring her out of there. Save her life!"

I shook my head. "You're talking big stuff here, Jenna. I don't know if we can and I don't know if we should."

Jenna ignored me, smiling into the mirror. "Sorrel says all I have to do is to put my hand into her time, and help her through."

"But what about this plague?" I asked. "Suppose she's already got it and she doesn't know it? Suppose she passes it on to us, and we pass it round the village and everyone dies, and then it goes on to the next town and round the world. . ."

"Don't be silly!" Jenna said impatiently.

"We've got proper medicines now, penicillin and all that. If Sorrel's actually got plague then she can be treated."

She put out her hand again towards the mirror. Her fingernails tapped gently on the glass and then – then, I swear! – her fingers moved through the glass and disappeared.

I gave a yelp of fright and pulled at her arm. "Jen! Hang on a minute!" I said.

"What's your problem?" Jenna turned a frowning face to me. "We can't just turn our backs on her. She needs us and we've got to help."

"But what if she pulls you through to *her* time?" I said. "How would I explain that to Mum? Oh sorry, Jenna's not here at the moment, she's just popped off to the seventeenth century. That'd go down well, wouldn't it?"

"Sorrel's not going to do that."

"How d'you know? And even if she doesn't, what are we supposed to do with her when she gets into our time? It's not right; it goes against the laws of . . . of something or other. Physics, I think," I added, frowning. "Anyhow, it's all wrong!"

But she wasn't even listening. "If we *can* help, we must," she said. "We can't just leave her to die!" and saying this her hand reached towards the mirror again. To my amazement I saw the glass part like water then close around it, and in the instant before it disappeared into the darkness I saw a thin, pale hand come to meet Jenna's, grasping firmly around her wrist. It was a small hand, but strong and bony, and it clutched at Jenna as if it would never let her go.

"No, you don't!" I said, and I flung my right arm round Jenna to pull her back from the mirror. At the same time I reached out with my left hand and punched the mirror to the floor.

There was an almighty crash, and then I distinctly heard two voices screaming, "No!" together. One of them was Jenna's, and I can only think that the other was Sorrel's. An instant later Jenna and I were sitting on the floor with slivers of broken mirror all around us.

"What did you do *that* for?" she said. "You've ruined everything! I could have saved her life! I could have brought her out of there."

"Never mind about *her*, you could have killed the rest of us!" I retorted.

Jenna looked at me, suddenly seeming to realize what had so nearly happened, and burst into tears.

CHAPTER EIGHT

"Well," I said, several days later, "if you *had* gone into that mirror, I s'pose I'd have just had to go in there after you and bring you back."

"Cheers," Jenna said.

"Not because I'd miss you or anything," I added hastily. "It's just that I couldn't have stood the aggro I'd have got from Mum."

"Well, cheers anyway."

We were walking across the green on our way to see the vicar, who'd left a message with Mum telling us to come over to the rectory (his big old house at the back of the church) because he had some information for us. On the way there the two of us had been going over what had happened in the pest house. And what *might* have happened in the pest house if I hadn't had the incredible presence of mind to whop the mirror at the last second.

"I wonder what happened to poor little Sorrel," Jenna said, sighing a bit.

"Never mind her," I said, because I'd already had two sleepless nights since it happened. "It's all over and done with now. Let's talk about something else. Football."

"Let's not."

"I don't believe you've ever mastered the offside rule. Now, a goal is only. . ."

But my efforts to educate the girl were rewarded by her putting her hands over her ears and running ahead of me, humming loudly.

"My husband's outside in the garden right now," the vicar's wife said when we knocked at the door of the rectory. "Do go on round."

I immediately pictured him out there talking to flowers, or doing something holy, but when we went round to the back we found him banging a ball against a wall. He wasn't bad, either.

He stopped when he saw us, tucked his white shirt into his black trousers and slicked back his three strands of hair. "Ah, hello," he said. "I've got some information on that project of yours. Come along in."

We followed him round the corner and through the tombstones into the church, where he had a little office containing a table with a whole mess of papers on it. "I found some most interesting details," he said, bending over and scrabbling in the papers like a ferret. "Now, where did I put them?"

After a bit more scrabbling, during which a lot of stuff got channelled on to the floor, he waved something at us triumphantly. "A copy of one of the Bills of Mortality for the month of September 1665," he said. "Take a look."

Finding a bit of free space on the table, he put down the paper and smoothed it out. It had an interestingly gruesome skull at the top of the page and then a long list of names and details, all written down in a funny script. I started reading out:

Died 14th September – William Struthers, Gamekeeper. Aged 43. Cause: Teeth.
Died 15th September – Alice May, Seamstress. Aged 38. Cause: Plague.

Died 15th September – Hannah Blake. Aged 10. Cause: Spotted Fever.

I looked down at all the causes of death. Most of them said plague, but there were some with strange things like, "Frighted" or "Rising of the Lights".

"What's that mean?" I asked, pointing at something called "Fits of the Mother".

"I've no idea," the vicar said, shaking his head. "They had illnesses we've never heard of. But look near the bottom of the page, though," he went on. "What can you see there?"

The handwriting changed here (the vicar said the clerk may have died of the plague halfway through the month) and wasn't so clear, so Jenna took the paper to the window to see it better. She read out: "*Died 25th September – Robin Wilson, Baker. Aged 27. Cause: Plague.*"

"And the next?" said the vicar.

Jenna gave a little gasp then turned to stare at us, startled.

"It's your girl, isn't it?" the vicar said.

Jenna nodded slowly. "The whole family are here," she said, lifting the paper to the light again. "On 26th September – Ellen and James

Larkin. Cause: plague. Then on 28th September, Grace Larkin aged nine, and Patience Larkin aged five, also of plague. And . . . and. . ." She looked at me and I could see she was about to start blubbing, so went to read it over her shoulder. "Died on 30th September. Sorrel Larkin, of plague," I finished for her.

We were all silent for quite a long time then – Jenna because she was choked and I because I just didn't know what to say. It was all real, then. Or it had been, once. Somehow we'd communicated with the seventeenth century.

"What you've got to remember," the vicar said, as Jenna dried her eyes on a bit of tissue, "is that it all happened a very long time ago. It's understandable that you should be sad when someone dies, but you didn't actually *know* the girl, did you?"

I gave Jenna a warning nudge.

"This is just a name on a piece of paper – nothing more than that."

"Well, I. . ." Jenna began between sniffs.

"Jenna's done quite a bit of research on the plague," I put in quickly, before she told him everything. "I think she feels –" here I gave a laugh – "as if she almost knew Sorrel. Had actually *seen* her."

"Ah. All very commendable," the vicar said vaguely. "But all things pass and life goes on, you know."

"Life goes on and ghosts go on as well," I said as we made our way back through the churchyard. "I wonder what sort of spook we'll find next."

Jenna put her hand on my arm. "D'you think we could go there just once more?"

"Where?"

"The pest house."

"You're kidding!" I yelped. "Haven't we seen enough of that place?"

She shrugged. "I really want to go there again. I don't know why. Just to put a finish to it all properly, I suppose."

"You're mad!"

"Just *see* the hut and say goodbye to Sorrel in my head. I don't even have to go inside. And we did say we'd get the pest house sign and take it to Ratty Ratcliffe for her history society, didn't we?"

I moaned and groaned a bit, and then I reminded her that she already owed me more favours than she could ever pay back in a lifetime. In the end, though, we struck some sort of deal involving loan of her TV for a week (which was newer and had a video with it) in exchange for going to the pest house instead of straight home.

Well, we *tried* to go to the pest house. What we actually did was go into Corpses' Copse and walk right through it until we came out the other side.

"We must have missed the clearing somehow," Jenna said, puzzled.

"It's you who usually knows where it is," I said. "Perhaps your psychic powers have deserted you."

"Let's have another try," she said, and we went right back to the starting-off point in Slurry Murray's field and began again.

With no luck.

"It's got to be here somewhere!" Jenna said, after we'd come out to the other side yet again without even seeing the pest house sign. One tree looked pretty much like another, though, they were all tall and brown, looming above and crowding around us. There was no sign of a hut. No sign, even, of a clearing between the trees.

"Everything seems kind of odd and empty," Jenna said, stopping and looking around. "It's like . . . after you get through a bad day at school or whatever and then it's all over and all you feel is emptiness and relief."

"Or like after the match when your team hasn't got relegated after all," I said helpfully. I rubbed my hands. "Come on, let's go," I said, bored with being there now. "And remember – it still counts. I did come to the wood with you, even if we didn't find the hut."

"What?" Jenna asked, sounding distracted.

We began walking back. "I still get to have a week's loan of your telly," I said.

"Of course!" she exclaimed, stopping suddenly.

I looked at her, surprised by the way she'd said it. She usually tries to wriggle out of stuff like that. "Yeah. A whole week. You agreed."

She stopped walking. "It *used* to be here!"

"What? What're you talking about?"

"The clearing was right here where we're standing. And the hut. But the hut's gone and the clearing's grown over." She shook my arm. "Look, Jake. The trees around us here are different. They're not so old as those big pine trees. *This* is where the clearing used to be."

I looked round. She could have been right. I don't know the names of trees but those around us were of a different type, not evergreen, and the darkness under them wasn't nearly as intense. "I bet if we look around a bit here, we'll find traces of where the hut used to be," she went on.

"Didn't the vicar say he thought it must have crumbled to bits?"

She nodded slowly, then she said, "I know this sounds crazy but what if . . . what if the whole hut was in some sort of time warp, and we just happened to come across it?"

"Do me a favour!"

"It could have been! The whole idea of what we've seen and heard – the mirror and the voices and everything – has been totally unbelievable. If it was in a time warp it makes a kind of sense."

"Yeah, but . . . but you just don't hear about stuff like that."

As I spoke, a wind moved through the trees, making a strange sighing noise. If you had a vivid imagination, it could have sounded like a group of people, moaning to themselves in despair.

"Did you hear that?" Jenna asked. "It sounded like. . ."

"It was just the wind," I said.

She closed her eyes a moment. "It was here. The hut was here – I know it was. Just where we're standing."

She stepped forward and it was then that I saw it. Straight out of a horror movie: a small, bony hand caked in grime snaking up from the ground to grab at Jenna's foot. It clutched at the toe of her trainers, but I was close enough to push her out of the way and she stumbled, almost fell over and the hand disappeared back into the earth.

"What did you do that for?" Jenna said, looking back at me crossly. "You nearly made me fall."

She hadn't seen it.

I thought quickly. "Just making you get a move on," I said. My hands were clammy and I pushed them deep into my pockets. "Look, there's nothing around here now," I said, steering her away. "Race you back to the field. If you win you can borrow my skateboard. If I win I can have your telly for *two* weeks."

She hesitated.

"I'll give you a start of ten seconds. Go on!"

She went. While I counted to ten (well, eight, actually, I didn't figure on losing and besides, there was no way I was hanging around there any longer than I had to) I looked closely at the ground where she'd been standing. There wasn't a trace of anything odd. Nothing that even *looked* like a hand.

OK, I might have imagined it.

But we never went back to Corpses' Copse again.